**This Book
Belongs to:**

~~Bruce J. Krug~~ (Bill)
Corbin Levi Semyak
from
Grandma Sandy
1998

"1988"

The Big Big Book of
MOTHER GOOSE

Favorite Rhymes Selected from the
Original Volland Edition

Original Illustrations by
FREDERICK RICHARDSON

DERRYDALE BOOKS
New York

FOREWORD

Derrydale Books is proud to present this beautiful edition containing selected Mother Goose rhymes chosen from the Original Volland Edition first published in 1915.

Collected here are the favorite rhymes of generations of children, accompanied by the glowing original illustrations created by Frederick Richardson. Among the many familiar characters to be found in this volume are Little Bo-peep, Little Boy Blue, Simple Simon, The Queen of Hearts, Little Miss Muffet, Jack and Jill, Little Tom Tucker, Humpty Dumpty, Old King Cole, Old Mother Hubbard—and, of course, Old Mother Goose herself.

This deluxe oversized edition is beautifully printed and bound in laminated paper over board to ensure long life. It is the perfect introduction for any child to the charmed realm of Mother Goose.

N.R.K.

New York City
1987

First published in 1987 by Derrydale Books,
distributed by Crown Publishers, Inc.,
225 Park Avenue South, New York, New York 10003

Manufactured in Italy

ISBN 0-517-64628-5
h g f e d c b a

Old Mother Goose, when
She wanted to wander,
Would ride through the air
On a very fine gander.

Peter, Peter, pumpkin eater,
Had a wife and couldn't keep her;
He put her in a pumpkin shell,
And then he kept her very well.

Peter, Peter, pumpkin eater,
Had another, and didn't love her;
Peter learned to read and spell,
And then he loved her very well.

Lady-bird, Lady-bird,
Fly away home,
Your house is on fire,
Your children will burn.

Little Bo-peep has lost her sheep,
And can't tell where to find them;
Leave them alone, and they'll come home,
And bring their tails behind them.

Jack, be nimble; Jack, be quick;
Jack, jump over the candlestick.

I'll tell you a story
  About Mary Morey,
And now my story's begun.
I'll tell you another
  About her brother,
And now my story's done.

Hush-a-bye, Baby, upon the tree top,
When the wind blows the cradle will rock;
When the bough breaks the cradle will fall,
Down tumbles cradle and Baby and all.

Dickery, dickery, dock,
The mouse ran up the clock;
The clock struck one,
The mouse ran down,
Dickery, dickery, dock.

A, B, C, D, E, F, G,
H, I, J, K, L, M, N, O, P,
Q, R, S, and T, U, V,
W, X, and Y and Z.
Now I've said my A, B, C,
Tell me what you think of me.

Bah, bah, black sheep,
　　Have you any wool?
Yes, marry, have I,
　　Three bags full;
One for my master,
　　One for my dame,
But none for the little boy
　　Who cries in the lane.

Wee Willie Winkie runs through the town,
Upstairs and downstairs, in his nightgown;
Tapping at the window, crying at the lock:
"Are the babes in their beds, for it's now ten o'clock?

There was an old woman who lived in a shoe,
She had so many children she didn't know what to do.
She gave them some broth without any bread,
She whipped them all soundly and put them to bed.

Simple Simon met a pieman
   Going to the fair;
Says Simple Simon to the pieman:
  "Pray let me taste your ware."

Says the pieman to Simple Simon:
  "Show me first your penny;"
Says Simple Simon to the pieman:
  "Indeed I have not any."

Sing a song of sixpence, a bag full of rye,
Four and twenty blackbirds baked in a pie;
When the pie was opened the birds began to sing,
And wasn't this a dainty dish to set before the king?
The king was in the parlor counting out his money;
The queen was in the kitchen eating bread and honey;
The maid was in the garden hanging out the clothes,
There came a little blackbird and nipped off her nose.

Little Miss Muffet
  Sat on a tuffet,
Eating some curds and whey;
  There came a great spider,
  And sat down beside her,
And frightened Miss Muffet away.

Bye, Baby bunting,
Father's gone a-hunting,
Mother's gone a-milking,
Sister's gone a-silking,
And Brother's gone to buy a skin
To wrap the Baby bunting in.

Tom, Tom, the piper's son,
Stole a pig, and away he run;
    The pig was eat,
    And Tom was beat,
And Tom ran crying down the street.

Jack and Jill went up the hill
  To fetch a pail of water;
Jack fell down and broke his crown,
  And Jill came tumbling after.

Pussy cat, pussy cat, where have you been?
I've been to London to see the Queen.
Pussy cat, pussy cat, what did you there?
I frightened a little mouse under the chair.

Pat a cake, pat a cake, Baker's man;
So I do, master, as fast as I can.
Pat it and prick it and mark it with T,
And then it will serve for Tommy and me.

Little Boy Blue, come blow your horn,
The sheep's in the meadow, the cow's in the corn.
What! Is this the way you mind your sheep,
Under the haycock fast asleep?

Little Tom Tucker
Sings for his supper.
What shall he eat?
White bread and butter.
How will he cut it
Without e`er a knife?
How will he marry
Without e`er a wife?

Diddle, diddle, dumpling, my son John,
Went to bed with his breeches on,
One stocking off, and one stocking on,
Diddle, diddle, dumpling, my son John.

High diddle diddle,
The cat and the fiddle,
The cow jumped over the moon;
The little dog laughed
To see such craft,
And the dish ran away with the spoon.

How many days has my baby to play?
    Saturday, Sunday, Monday,
    Tuesday, Wednesday, Thursday, Friday,
    Saturday, Sunday, Monday.

Humpty Dumpty sat on a wall,
Humpty Dumpty had a great fall;
All the king's horses and all the king's men
Couldn't put Humpty Dumpty together again.

Little Jack Horner
  Sat in a corner
Eating a Christmas pie;
  He put in his thumb,
  And pulled out a plum,
And said: "Oh, what a good boy am I!"

The Queen of Hearts,
She made some tarts
All on a summer's day;
The Knave of Hearts,
He stole those tarts,
And took them clean away.

The King of Hearts
Called for the tarts,
And beat the Knave full sore;
The Knave of Hearts
Brought back the tarts,
And vowed he'd steal no more.

Goosey, goosey, gander, where dost thou wander?
Upstairs and downstairs and in my lady's chamber;
There I met an old man that wouldn't say his prayers,
I took him by his hind legs and threw him downstairs.

See saw, Margery Daw,
   Jacky shall have a new master:
Jacky must have but a penny a day
Because he can work no faster.

Old King Cole
Was a merry old soul,
And a merry old soul was he;
He called for his pipe,
And he called for his bowl,
And he called for his fiddlers three.

Mistress Mary, quite contrary,
How does your garden grow?
With silver bells and cockle shells
And pretty maids all in a row.

This pig went to market,
That pig stayed at home;
This pig had roast meat,
That pig had none;
This pig went to the barn door,
And cried "week, week," for more.

Old Mother Hubbard
Went to the cupboard
   To get her poor dog a bone;
But when she came there
The cupboard was bare,
   And so the poor dog had none.

Pease-porridge hot,
  Pease-porridge cold,
Pease-porridge in the pot
  Nine days old.
Spell me that in four letters:
  I will: T H A T.

Polly, put the kettle on,
Polly, put the kettle on,
Polly, put the kettle on,
  We'll all have tea.
Sukey, take it off again,
Sukey, take it off again,
Sukey, take it off again,
  They're all gone away.

Jack Sprat could eat no fat.
  His wife could eat no lean;
So 'twixt them both they cleared the cloth,
  And licked the platter clean.

There was a crooked man,
    And he went a crooked mile,
He found a crooked sixpence
    Against a crooked stile;
He bought a crooked cat
    Which caught a crooked mouse,
And they all lived together
    In a little crooked house.